Good For Me
Vegetables

Sally Hewitt

PowerKiDS press.

New York

Notes for Teachers and Parents

Good for Me is a series of books that looks at ways of helping children to develop a positive approach to eating. You can use the books to help children make healthy choices about what they eat and drink as an important part of a healthy lifestyle.

Look for vegetables when you go shopping.
- Look at the different types of vegetables in your local supermarket.
- Read the ingredients on packages to see if the food contains vegetables.
- Buy something new. Have fun preparing it and eating it with children.

Talk about different food groups and how we need to eat a variety of foods from each group every day.
- Vegetables are packed with vitamins, minerals, and fiber.
- Talk about the ways vitamins, minerals, and fiber help to keep us strong and healthy.

Talk about how we feel when we are healthy, and the things we can do to help us to stay healthy.
- Eat food that is good for us.
- Drink plenty of water.
- Enjoy fresh air and exercise.
- Sleep well.

Published in 2008 by The Rosen Publishing Group, Inc.
29 East 21st Street, New York, NY 10010

Copyright © 2008 Wayland/The Rosen Publishing Group, Inc.

First Edition

Produced by Tall Tree Ltd.
Editor: Jon Richards
Designer: Ben Ruocco
Consultant: Sally Peters

Library of Congress Cataloging-in-Publication Data

Hewitt, Sally, 1949—
  Vegetables / Sally Hewitt. — 1st ed.
    p. cm. — (Good for me)
  Includes index.
  ISBN 978-1-4042-4265-4 (library binding)
  1. Vegetables—Juvenile literature. 2. Cookery (Vegetables)—Juvenile
literature. I. Title.
  TX401.H49 2008
  641.6'51—dc22
                        2007032507

Manufactured in China

Picture credits:
Cover top Corbis/Tim Pannell, bottom Dreamstime.com/Sasha Radosavljevic, 4 Alamy/The Anthony Blake Photo Library, 5 Dreamstime.com, 6 Alamy/Stock Connection Distribution, 7 Dreamstime.com/Paul Cowan, 8 Dreamstime.com/Sasha Radosavljevic, 9 Dreamstime.com, 10 Dreamstime.com, 11 Corbis, 12 Still Pictures/Sean Sprague, 13 Dreamstime.com/Dianne Maire, 14 Dreamstime.com, 15 Alamy/Keyfoto, 16 Alamy/allover photography, 17 Dreamstime.com/Florea Marius Catalin, 18 Alamy/Foodfolio, 19 Bubbles Photolibrary/Claire Camm, 20 center Dreamstime.com, bottom left Dreamstime.com, bottom middle Dreamstime.com, bottom right Dreamstime.com/Andy Butler, 21 top middle Dreamstime.com, center left Dreamstime.com, upper center Alamy/Foodfolio, center right Dreamstime.com/Lorelyn Medina, center Dreamstime.com/Andrei Dragut, bottom left Alamy/Foodfolio, bottom center Dreamstime.com/Olga Lyubkina, bottom right Dreamstime.com/Paul Cowan 23 Corbis/Tim Pannell

Contents

Good for me

Everyone needs to eat food and drink water to live, grow, and be **healthy**. All the food we eat comes from animals and plants. Vegetables are food from plants.

We eat **roots**, stalks, leaves, and the flowers of plants. Carrots are roots.

You can grow
vegetables in
a vegetable
plot or in a
pot with some
soil and water.

Vegetables are grown on farms and in pots
and plots. They need rain and sunshine to
grow and ripen. Vegetables are delicious to
eat. They are good for you!

Healthy vegetables

Vegetables are full of **vitamins** and **minerals**. Every part of your body needs vitamins and minerals to be **healthy** and to fight **germs**.

Eating vegetables helps to keep you active.

You need to chew crunchy vegetables very well because they are full of **fiber**. Fiber is important. It helps your body get rid of unwanted food.

Lunchbox

Sticks of **raw** carrot and celery are healthy to eat.

You should eat five **portions** of fresh vegetables and fruit every day.

Roots and bulbs

Roots and **bulbs** are the parts of plants that grow underground. They are large, because this is where the plant stores the food it needs to grow. You can eat the roots and bulbs of many plants.

Carrots, potatoes, sweet potatoes, yams, parsnips, turnips, and radishes are all root vegetables.

Onions grow in many layers, which you can see when they are chopped up.

Onions and garlic are bulbs with a strong taste. We use them to flavour salads, soups and stews. Be careful, chopping onions can make you cry.

Lunchbox

Ask an adult to warm some vegetable soup. Put it in a thermos for lunch.

Leaves, flowers, and fruit

Plants make food from sunlight in their green leaves. Cabbages, lettuces, and spinach all grow leaves that we can eat.

Cauliflower really is a flower. We eat the white flower and not the leaves.

We often call cucumbers, tomatoes, and peppers vegetables, but they are fruit. Fruit is the part of the plant where seeds are made.

Can you see the seeds inside peppers when they are cut open?

Lunchbox

Vegetables have interesting shapes. Ask an adult to cut circles of raw bell peppers to eat.

Growing vegetables

Vegetables grow all over the world, all year round. Some types of vegetable grow where it is warm and wet, others grow where it is hot and dry.

Yams grow in Central America and the Caribbean, where it is hot and sunny.

In mild countries, vegetables such as lettuces are grown in greenhouses all year round.

Vegetables grow in **greenhouses** in all kinds of weather. Inside a greenhouse, plants are given the water, sunlight, and the heat they need to grow.

Lunchbox

Use different types of leaves, such as spinach and arugula, to make salads.

Buying and storing

Most vegetables should be kept cool and eaten soon after buying. Root vegetables should be stored in a dry, dark place. We buy fresh vegetables at a farm store or a supermarket.

Fresh vegetables are delivered to supermarkets every day.

Vegetables can be frozen, canned, or dried so that they last. Frozen vegetables stored in the freezer keep for about three months. Canned and dried vegetables will last for more than a year.

Canned vegetables are stored in water or juice to make them last.

Lunchbox

If you run out of fresh vegetables, you can add canned carrots and green beans to your salad.

Raw vegetables

Bright-colored raw vegetables are full of vitamins and minerals. The fresher they are, the more goodness there is inside them. Wash raw vegetables and chew them well.

Eating crunchy raw vegetables helps to keep your teeth healthy and strong.

This salad uses red, yellow, and green vegetables.

You can make different-colored salads. Lettuce, green pepper, and cucumber make a green salad. Tomatoes, red bell pepper, and radish make a red salad. Carrots and orange peppers make an orange salad.

Lunchbox

See how many different colors you can have in the salads you make for your school lunchbox.

17

Cooked vegetables

Vegetables can be eaten cooked as well as raw. If vegetables are cooked too much, they lose some of their goodness. Cooked vegetables should keep their fresh, bright color.

Steamed vegetables, such as carrots and broccoli, should still be crunchy.

Root vegetables can be boiled and mashed, baked, or roasted. The skins are good to eat if you scrub them clean.

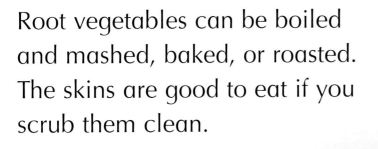

Lunchbox

Ask an adult to roast thin slices of root vegetables with a sprinkle of olive oil and a little salt. Eat them instead of potato chips.

Baked potatoes are healthy, especially if you eat the skins.

Food chart

Here are some examples of foods that can be made using three types of vegetables. Have you tried any of these?

Potato

Baked potato

Mashed potato

Boiled potatoes

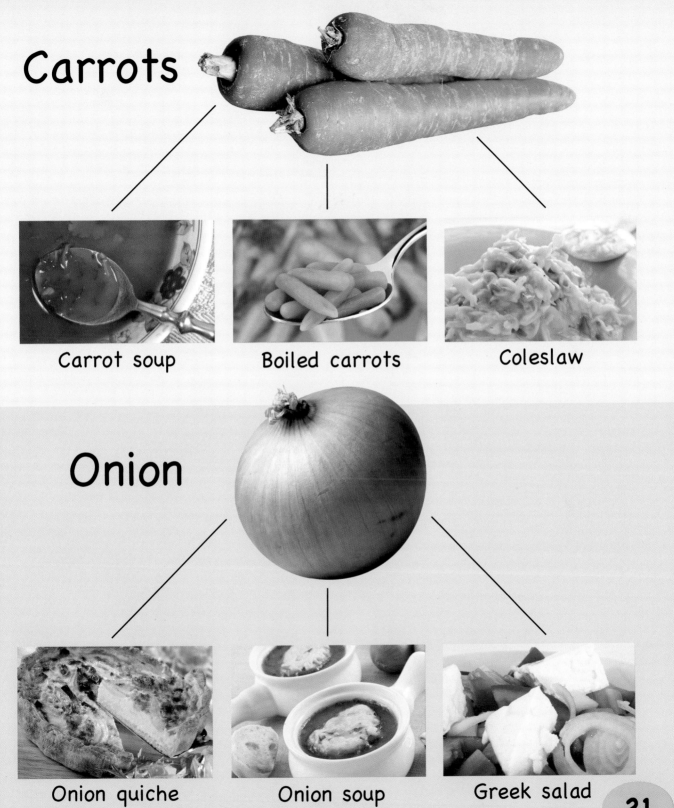

Carrots

Carrot soup

Boiled carrots

Coleslaw

Onion

Onion quiche

Onion soup

Greek salad

21

A balanced diet

This chart shows you how much you can eat of each food group. The larger the area on the chart, the more of that food group you can eat. For example, you can eat a lot of fruit and vegetables, but only a little oil and sweets. Drink plenty of water every day, too.

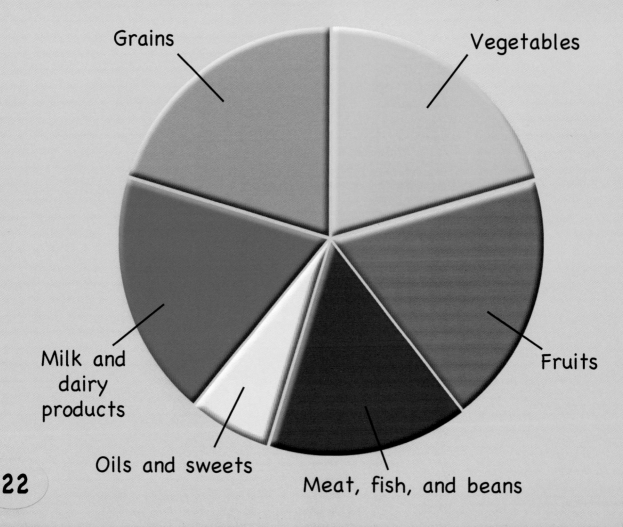

Grains

Vegetables

Milk and dairy products

Fruits

Oils and sweets

Meat, fish, and beans

Our bodies also need exercise to stay healthy. You should spend at least 20 minutes exercising every day, so that your body stays fit and healthy.

Taking part in organized sports is a great way to stay fit.

Glossary

Bulbs The swollen parts of a root where some plants, such as onions, store the food they need to grow.

Fiber The rough part of fruit. It helps your body to get rid of any unwanted food.

Germs Tiny creatures that can be harmful and can make you sick.

Greenhouses Houses made of glass or plastic for growing plants that need sunshine, heat, and protection from the weather.

Healthy When you are fit and not sick.

Minerals Important substances that are found in food. Calcium is a mineral that helps to build strong bones.

Portion This is the amount of food a person should eat.

Raw Not cooked.

Roots The part of a plant that grows beneath the ground.

Vitamins Substances found in food that help our bodies stay healthy. For example, vitamin D helps you to grow strong bones.

Index